Wilbur's
Epic Journey

by
Dione

ISBN (PB): 978-1-961497-28-3

Dedication

To the curious and adventurous kids of the world, who possess the boundless imagination and fearlessness to explore and learn. May you always find inspiration in the stories of nature's wonders and the resilience of its creatures. May you grow with the understanding of the interconnectedness of all life and embrace the beauty and lessons that surround you. May your hearts be filled with compassion and your spirits forever wild and free.

Acknowledgement

I would like to express my deepest gratitude to everyone, especially my daughters, who supported me throughout the journey of crafting this story. Your encouragement, belief in my abilities, and unwavering support have been invaluable. I am immensely thankful to my editor and publisher for their guidance and expertise in shaping this book. Your dedication to excellence and meticulous attention to detail have truly brought this story to life.

Lastly, I want to extend my heartfelt thanks to my readers. Your interest, engagement, and enthusiasm for my work have touched me profoundly. It is an honour to have you join me on this literary adventure. Thank you all for being an integral part of this journey with me.

And whatever you do, whether in word or deed, do it all in the name of the Lord Jesus, giving thanks to God the Father through him. Colossians 3 :17

About the Author

Wilbur's Epic Journey is Dione Butcher's first book. Dione has always had a deep love for science and takes great pleasure in trying to convince people that science is fun and helps us understand how nature works. Dione was born in London but grew up in Guyana. On her return to London, she obtained a degree in Chemistry and worked in the food industry for 23 years. She retrained as a science teacher after being made redundant and found that she loved to share her knowledge of nature and science in a fun and accessible way. She derived great pleasure from seeing young people show understanding and appreciation of nature and natural phenomena because of how she would break down complicated concepts so that they are more relevant to them. Dione was looking for a book about migration of animals and couldn't find one that very young children could engage with so she decided to write Wilbur's Epic journey. She has continued to use her skill of patiently explaining natural events in a fun way with this book.

Wilbur hit the ground
with a bump. He laid on
the soft grass taking in
the new smells and
sounds around him;

slowly responding to the
gentle prodding of his
mum as she encouraged
him to stand.

Wildebeest calves must be able to stand and walk very soon after they are born.

Wilbur is a wildebeest calf born on the Serengeti Plains in Tanzania in

AFRICA

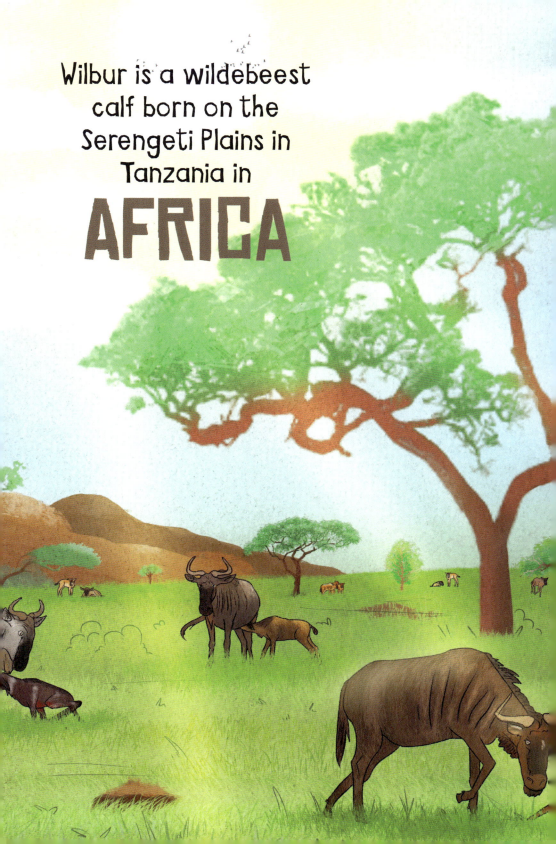

This is the birthing season for wildebeests and many other animals who live here because there is a good supply of food. Wilbur is one of about a half a million wildebeest calves who will be born between January and March.

Wilbur tried to stand but kept slipping and falling over.

But very soon he got the hang of it.

He stood tall gazing out at the majesty of the vast green Serengeti Plains and all the animals and plants around him.

In no time at all he was running with the other wildebeest calves but being careful to stay close to his mum.

Wilbur loves munching on the sweet grass.

Wilbur loves
playing and skipping

Wilbur is growing fast and
learning so much.
The herds are always on the
move, so he and the other
calves must keep up.

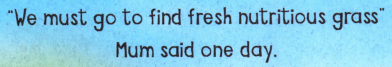

"We must go to find fresh nutritious grass"
Mum said one day.

"Where is that Mum?" Wilbur asked.

"Take a deep breath," she said, "can you smell that?"

"Yes, that's smells fresh. It's making me feel hungry."

Wilbur and mum laughed.

"That's the smell of rain.
Can you see the dark clouds over there in
the distance?"

asked Mum.

"That is where the rain is and where fresh green grass will soon start to grow after it rains. That's where we are heading."

"Aww, I'm going to miss my friends."

said Wilbur.

"Oh no you won't." replied Mum. "They are all coming with us. We do this every year. We move from one place to another to find good nutritious grass. It's called a migration. So, please stay close to me. It could be a very dangerous time."

"Yes Mum." Wilbur called as he ran off to play.

Suddenly there was a stampede, and everyone scattered. Wilbur looked around but he was alone.
"Muuummm!" screamed Wilbur.
But he couldn't see her.

WILBUR WAS SCARED!!
It was absolute pandemonium. Animals were running here, there, and everywhere.

Wilbur glanced around at the animal chasing him. Time froze. That glance felt like a whole hour had passed. He did not know this animal, but he knew he was scared of it. He had seen it in the distance but never so close up. This one did not look friendly. It had long, sharp pointed teeth and looked at him with menacing eyes.

This was a lion!

Instinctively, he knew he had to get away from it.

Wilbur bolted off not knowing
where he was going.
And the lion was chasing him.

His little legs were aching.
His chest was burning because
he was running so fast.

Still the lion chased him.
Wilbur's little legs were
moving him this way and
that as he gave that lion
the slip.

Suddenly there was another set of **thundering footsteps** as Mum raced to help Wilbur.

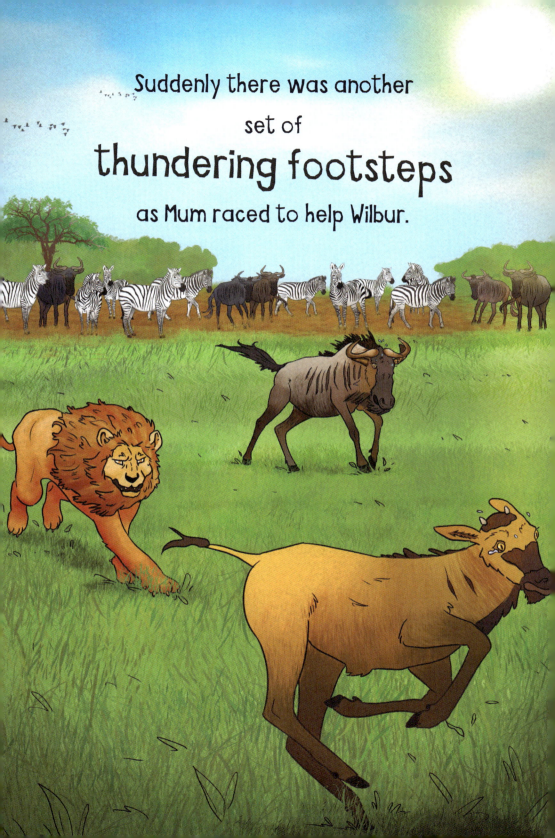

Then a dark flash as she
whizzed past
Wilbur and......!

a thump when Mum **head butted** the lion, followed by a loud wail when the lion was thrown into the air.

Wilbur kept on running.
Someone was calling
his name.
"WILBUR!"
"Huh."
Wilbur
screeched to halt when
he recognised Mum's
voice.

"WILBUR!"
it was Mum.
"Mum."
Wilbur ran to his mum.
"Come quickly,
let's go back to the herd.

We must stick together if
we are to stay safe." Mum explained.

Wilbur and his mum ran back to the herd,
and they continued their journey towards
the rain and fresh nutritious grass.

On their way back to the herd, Wilbur asked
Mum about what had just happened.
"They wait for us at this time. They need
to eat just like we do, and they also have
little ones that they need to find food for."
Mum explained to Wilbur.

"Do you mean...?" Wilbur couldn't bring himself
to finish the question.
"Yes," replied Mum. "We are food for them."
Wilbur gulped, his eyes opened wide.
"It's the 'cycle of life' my son." said Mum and
she explained this to Wilbur.

"Every living thing needs energy and nutrients to live a healthy life and we get those from the food we eat. We eat grass to give us energy, but do you know that the grass makes its own food?"
"Really!" chimed in Wilbur.
"Yes, it uses energy from the sun with rainwater and carbon dioxide from the air to make food for itself. Then, when you eat grass, it gives you energy to run and play.
Lions need energy too, so they eat us. And vultures eat lions when they die to get the energy they need. Everything goes into the ground when it dies and then that becomes nutrients for the grass which makes it grow healthy and tasty for us. So, you see, we need each other to stay alive."
"Wow!" marvelled Wilbur. "I didn't know that. That's very interesting."
"That's why it is important to stay alert to everything going on around you and always stay with the herd, so you don't end up as lunch for a hungry animal."
Mum warned him.
"You are so right Mum."

Cycle of Life

Wilbur looked around for his friends, but he could not find them. He so wanted to tell them about his adventure.

"You will make new friends along the way." said Mum.
"This sort of thing happens all the time. Soon we will reach the new grass where we will stop and graze for a time. You might be able to find them then."

The herds moved along the Serengeti
plains on their epic journey stopping
to graze occasionally.
Wilbur made new friends.

Mum seems to be a bit busy too.
Well, all the grown-ups are getting
together more now as this is the start
of the mating season when the males
and females get together to mate.

One day Mum called out to him,
"Wilbur, stay
close now. We are at the river."
"Oh! What's a river?" asked Wilbur.
"Come and see," said Mum.
The herds have now arrived at the

Mara River.

When they cross this river, they
would be
in another country in Africa.
She led Wilbur to the riverbank.

Wilbur stood next to mum
taking in the scene when
suddenly there was a splash

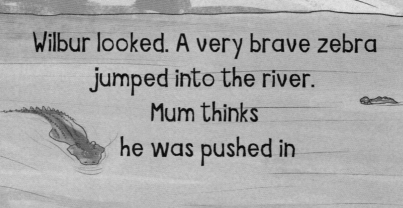

Wilbur looked. A very brave zebra
jumped into the river.
Mum thinks
he was pushed in

"Is that how you swim, Mum?"
Wilbur asked as he watched
the zebra in the river.

"Yes, but you must be quick. Look, see the crocodiles?" Wilbur gasped, his eyes and mouth wide open with fear.

A crocodile was heading straight for the zebra. "Mum," Wilbur asked, "is this 'the cycle of life' again?"

"Yes Wilbur. You really are learning your life's lessons well." said Mum proudly. As they were talking, they heard it. It started as a low, slow chant. "Faster! Faster! Faster!"

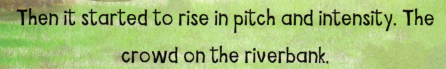

Then it started to rise in pitch and intensity. The crowd on the riverbank, watching the crocodile approach the zebra in the water, were egging him on.

"Faster! Faster! Faster!"

The zebra didn't look back.
He looked straight
ahead and swam
as fast as he could to the
opposite bank.

Soon, he scrambled up the bank just out of reach of the crocodile's snapping jaws.

Now, those at the back of the herd, heard the chanting and wanted to know what was going on, so they were crowding in closer and closer, pushing Wilbur and his mum closer and closer to the water.

"Whoa!" screamed Wilbur.
"This is it."
said Mum "Be careful,
see you on the other side."

Wilbur followed mum and skipped down the
riverbank. He and Mum jumped into the water
with other wildebeests and zebras to
cross over to Kenya.
When he reached the water, it just happened.
He swam.
His legs were much stronger now from eating
all the nutritious grass and running and
playing and skipping.

"Keep your head up Wilbur and keep your legs moving." he said to encourage himself.
"Keep going, you've got this." Wilbur kept going surrounded by the heaving dark bodies of wildebeests all around him.
He felt safe.

Soon, he could feel the ground under his feet again. He clambered up the bank to safety and heard someone calling his name.

"Wilbur! Wilbur! Where are you, Wilbur?"

Wilbur recognised the voice
instantly.
"Mum! Mum!" he called back
and ran in
the direction of her voice.
"Mum!"

They found each other.
What a relief.

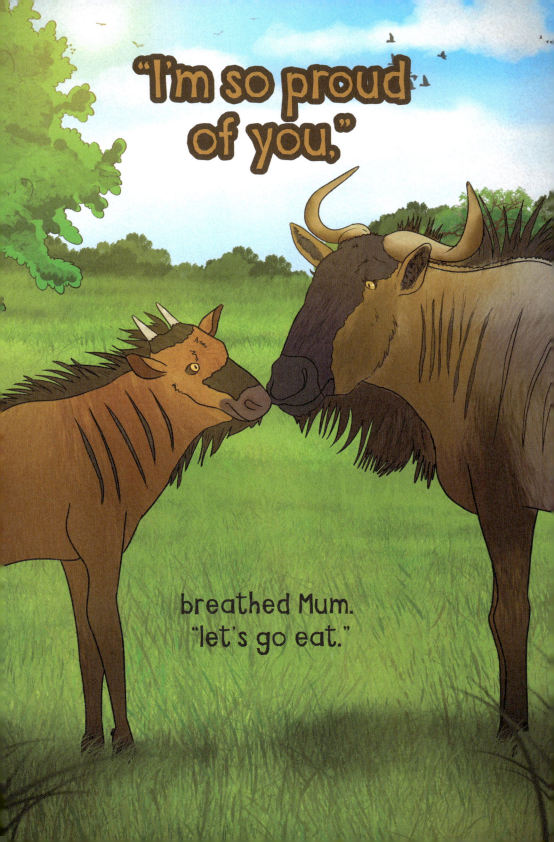

Wilbur made lots of new friends too. He was feeling more confident now and didn't want to be with his mum all the time. One day he went to play with his friends and when he returned, he couldn't find her.

"Oh well," Wilbur shrugged his shoulders and went off again with his friends.

Mum was watching from a distance among a group of other wildebeests.
She smiled to herself when she saw that her little Wilbur was now confident to face the world without her. Her heart swelled with pride mixed with a hint of sadness.
The other wildebeest told her "He will be fine. They will all be okay."

Wilbur and Mum and the huge herds grazed on the great, stunning plains of the Masai Mara in Kenya, where he continued to learn and grow.

The herds grazed on the Masai Mara
feasting on the green grass rich in all
kinds of goodness,
making them
healthier and stronger
Since they left the Serengeti,
the rains came, and fresh new tender
shoots of grass have
started to grow there again.

The females are pregnant, and they want to go back there so their calves will have soft nutritious grass to feed on when they are born.

Soon the animals were beginning to gather
from all over plains to form their
great herds and set off on their
journey back to the Serengeti.

Wilbur and his friends stayed in the middle of the herd as they headed back to the Mara river.

Soon they reached the river and swam back to Tanzania. Wilbur was much more confident this time as he knew what to expect. He even noticed that the water felt cool and refreshing, something he hadn't noticed before.

Wilbur was even thinking
how much he
actually enjoys swimming.
Then he smiled to himself, "Not in here
with all these hungry crocodiles."

Soon he was climbing up the riverbank
unto the Serengeti plains.

Wilbur and his friends wandered
the great plains together.

They were all growing in strength and
confidence knowing they will have to
make this journey all over again...

VERY SOON.

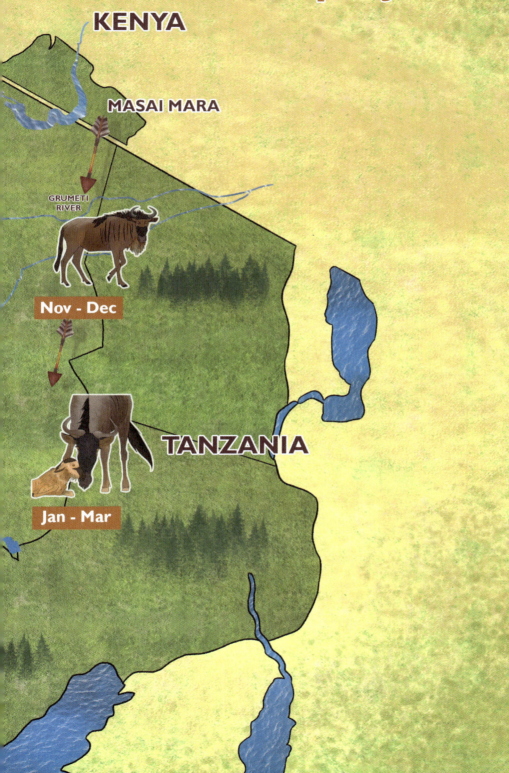

Wilbur's Epic Journey

KENYA

MASAI MARA

GRUMETI
RIVER

Nov - Dec

TANZANIA

Jan - Mar

Moral Of the Story

Life is a journey. Along the way, we may face obstacles that could put us in danger, but we must push forward through it and not give up. We have the courage and strength in us that will enable us to conquer our fears and problems. The people in our lives are there to support us in difficult times and make our happy moments even more memorable so it is right that we value and appreciate them.

Printed in Great Britain
by Amazon

43338046R00046